Upside-Downers

Hello! We're jokers,
upside-downers
from the
land of cards.
We say saw
when you say see.

So when you play
see-saw, we
play saw-see.

Won't you come and joke with us?
We'll swing and sing
and stand on our hands.
Peep through your legs,
put your head where your feet are,
and then you'll be
as upside down as we are!

Up side, down side—sing and swing side!
Front side, back side—hand and stand side!
Right side, left side—head and feet side!

Here's a house of cards—
all inside-out,
all upside-down.
And in it sleep
the kings' own soldiers—
all snoring and kicking,
all rolling and tossing.
Don't open the door!
Don't dare wake them!

They're snoring and snicking and kicking and koring,
they're rolling and rossing and tossing and tolling,
they're snossing and rolling and ricking and toring.

7

Didn't I say don't open the pack!
Now the king's own soldiers—
are inside out!

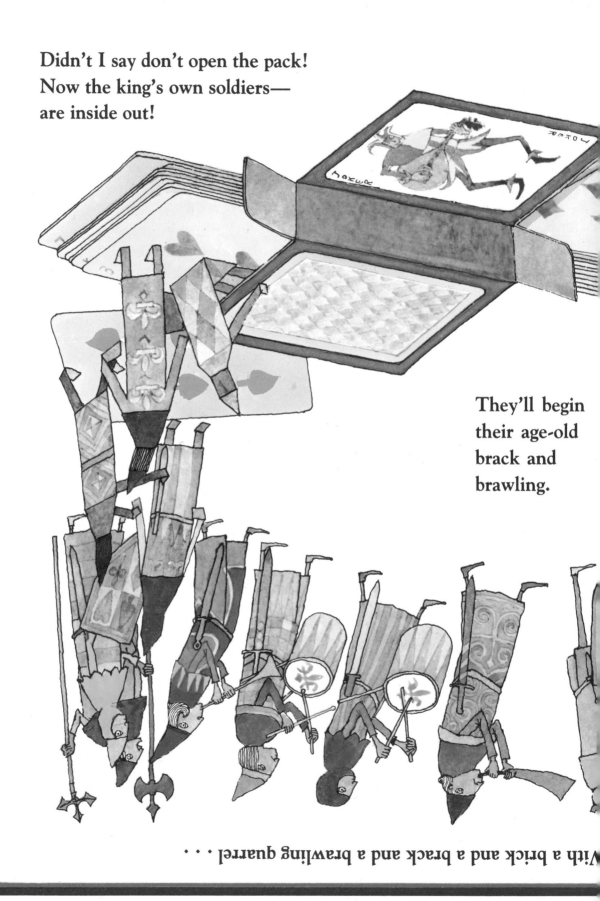

They'll begin
their age-old
brack and
brawling.

With a brick and a brack and a brawling quarrel . . .

8

They'll begin
their queer
and quacky
quarreling.

**Rustling hustlers
and hustling rustlers . . .**

**Rumbling grumblers
and grumbling rumblers . . .**

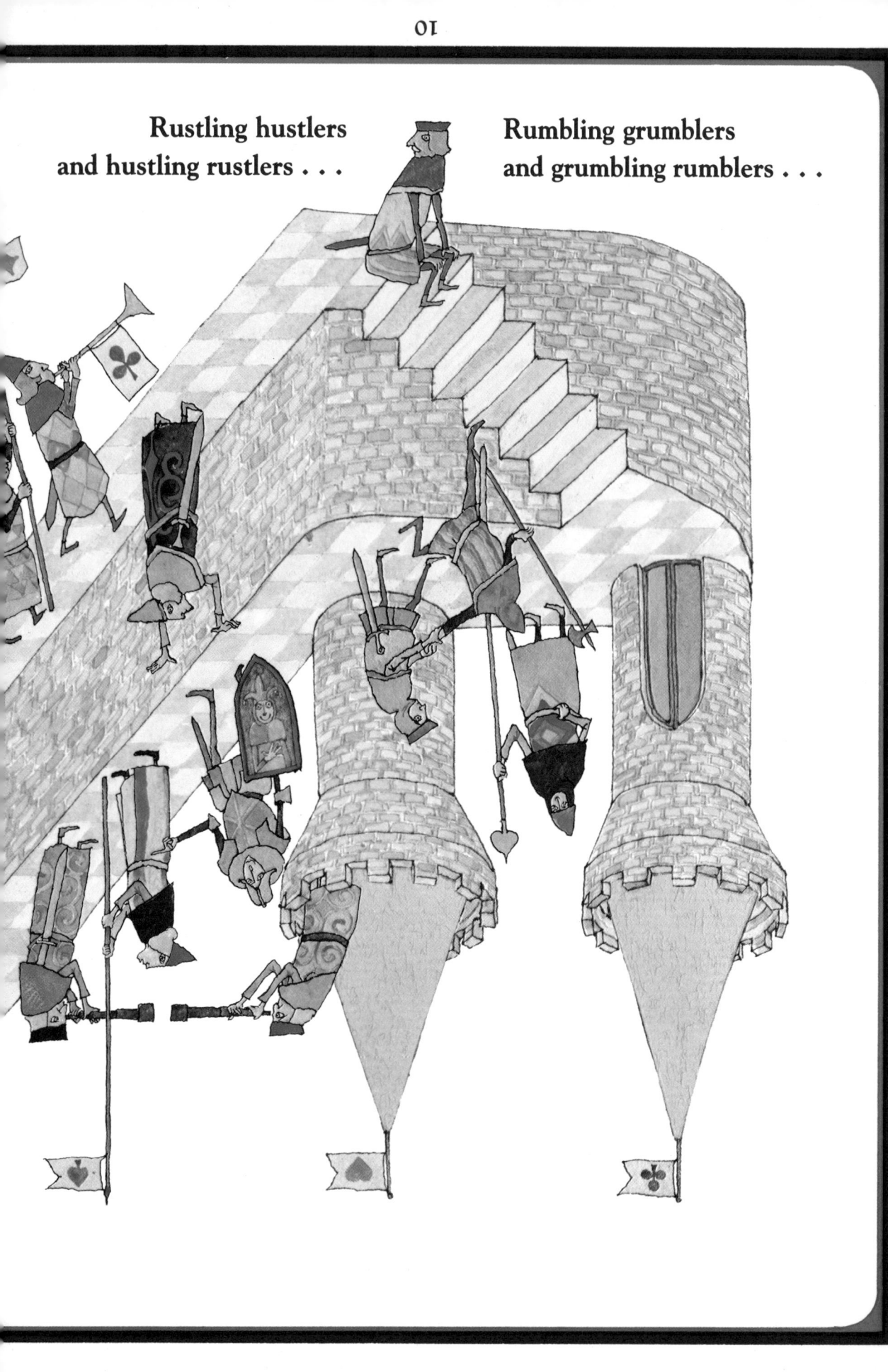

Rustle, hustle—they go bustling.
Rumble, tumble—they start grumbling.
"Hey! You're upside-down, you clown!"
"No, it's you who's wrong way round!"

So it goes
and so it's gone
for hundreds
and
hundreds
of years.

Up is down and down is up;
and rain falls from the ground:

"Hey! It's raining here," they cry.

We splash and we squirt, we paddle and puddle.
We rustle and bustle and grumble and rumble.

"Hey! It's raining *here*," they cry.

"A boat in the sky—that's crazy!"
"Houses in clouds—that's mad!"
"You're upside-down, you big baboons!"
"You're downside-up, you silly loons!"

Now listen to me,
you up-down things:
Stop quarreling or
I'll tell your kings!

"You're crazy, you're mad, you big baboons!"
"You're zany, you're sad, you silly loons!"

Hurry, hurry—no more bickering!
Scurry, scurry—no more dickering!

What a good idea!
What an excellent plan!
Let the kings decide.
On to the castle,
and hurray for our side.

To reach the throne-room
you go through a
drafty-wafty hallway,
up a twisty-turny
staircase, through a
crazy-mazy chamber—
No, wait a minute . . .
it's *down* you go
. . . or is it, *up*?
Well, anyway,
keep going,
and then . . .

We're all mixed up—
for down is up.
We're all mixed down—
for up is down.

se on your face?   Be an ace, Your Grace! Put them in their place!"

'O King, Great King,
Your Heartiness,
aren't *we* the ones who are up?"
'O King, Kind King,
Your Clubbiness,
aren't *they* the ones who are down?"

"Now isn't it as plain as t

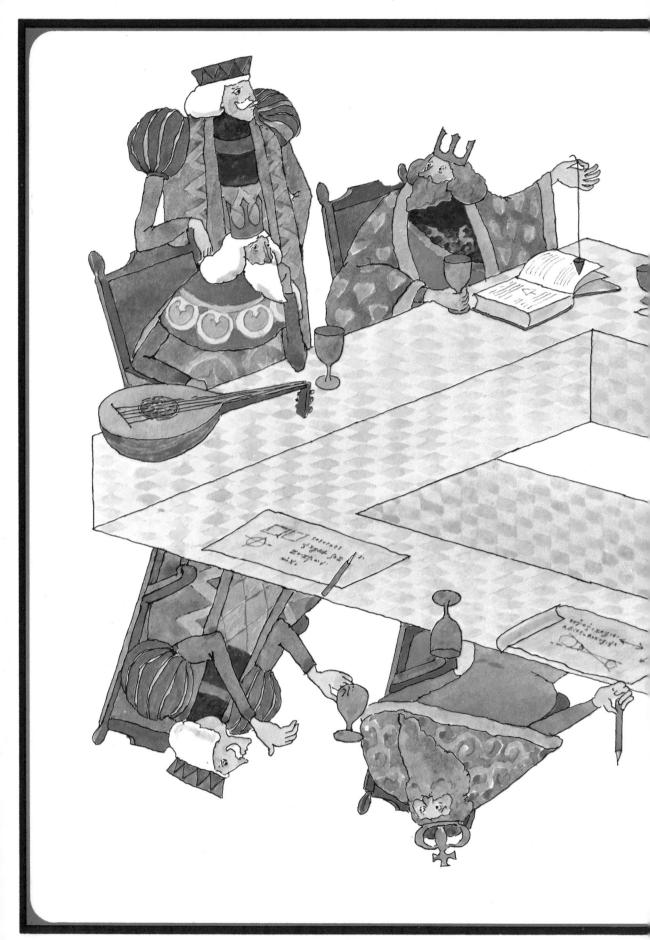

Four great kings—or are
there eight?—have wondered
and pondered and pulled
their beards these hundreds
and hundreds of years.
But still they don't know,
they just can't decide,
which side is upside
and which side is down.
They—just—can't—tell!

If upside is downside, and cup-side
is sup-side, if down-side is crown-side,
and gown-side is town-side;
then come-side is go-side,
and high-side
is low-side,
and in-side
is out-side,
and each side
is no-side.

Then one old king has
a new idea: "It's all
in your point of view,"
says he. "If there's
up, there's down. If
there's you, there's
me. For the world is
round, you see. So
please stop bickering
and come with me;
please stop grumbling
and let's go see."

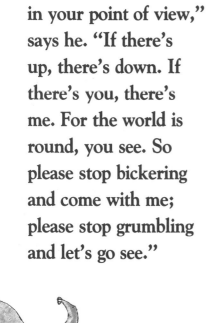

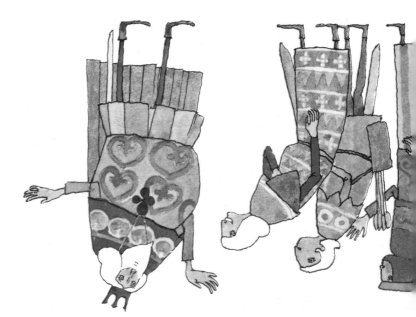

This point of view
is something new!
Can flat
be round?
Can up
be down?

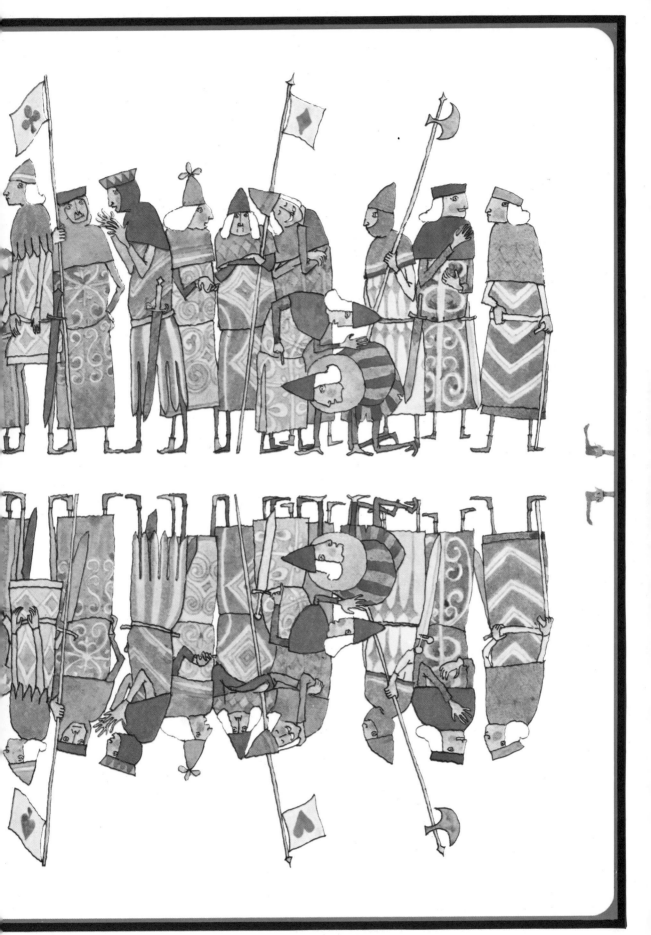

Can this be the end?
Well, maybe so.
But the world is round
and if up can be down
then ends can be
beginnings.

So away they go with the smart old king
to look at some points of view.
They march through cities and towns,
through woods and plains and summer rains.
They march and march and march again,
all the way around the world,
looking at points of view.

And now they know the answer.
Do you know it too?
Which side is upside
and which side is downside?
What's your point of view?

AUTHOR'S POSTSCRIPT

I hope that this will cause wonder.
For I still and always believe that one is never
too young, or too old, to begin learning how wide
a little imagination can stretch the joy of living.
In this book, a child can sit opposite his mother
or father and they can both read the book to each other
at the same time. Others may want to read the book
for themselves, maybe by going through it one way and
then turning it around and going back the other way.
That's fine too. Because this is a book without any rules.
It's simply to be enjoyed and perhaps
wondered over a little.

—Mitsumasa Anno

New American edition published in 1988 by Philomel Books, a division of The Putnam & Grosset
Group, 51 Madison Avenue, New York, NY 10010. First English edition published in 1971 by
John Weatherhill, Inc., New York and Tokyo. Original copyright © 1969 and 1971 Kūsō-Kōbō.
First published in 1969 by Fukuinkan Shoten Publishers, Tokyo. All rights reserved.
Printed in Japan. First impression

Library of Congress Cataloging-in-Publication Data Anno, Mitsumasa, date. Upside-downers /
Mitsumasa Anno. p. cm. Summary: Figures from two sets of playing cards, each of which seems
upside down to the other, pursue their queer and quacky quarreling, until one of the kings points out
that it is all a matter of point of view. ISBN 0-399-21522-0 [1. Cards—Fiction. 2. Perspective
(Philosophy)—Fiction.] I. Title. PZ7.A5875Up 1988 [E]—dc19 87-19850 CIP AC